The Magic School Bus
On the Ocean Floor

BUS ROUTES TO THE SOUTH PACIFIC

Ocean Notions

Sails Snails & Whales

She Sells Seashells Down by the Seashore

The Magic School Bus

On the Ocean Floor

By Joanna Cole / Illustrated by Bruce Degen

Scholastic Inc.

New York · Toronto · London · Auckland · Sydney
Mexico City · New Delhi · Hong Kong · Buenos Aires

ISBN-13: 978-0-590-41431-9
ISBN-10: 0-590-41431-3

Text copyright © 1992 by Joanna Cole.
Illustrations copyright © 1992 by Bruce Degen.
All rights reserved. Published by Scholastic Inc.

SCHOLASTIC, THE MAGIC SCHOOL BUS and associated logos are trademarks
and/or registered trademarks of Scholastic Inc.

31 30 29 28   13 14 15 16/0

Printed in the U.S.A.   08

The illustrator used pen and ink, watercolor, color pencil,
and gouache for the paintings in this book.

The ocean animals and plants are labeled only at their first appearance within the story.

*The author and illustrator wish to thank John D. Buck, Ph.D.,
Professor of Marine Sciences, Marine Science Institute, The University
of Connecticut, for his assistance in preparing this book.*

*For their helpful advice and consultation, thanks also to
Dr. Susan Snyder, Program Director, Teacher Preparation and
Enrichment, National Science Foundation; Dr. Michael Reeve, Division of
Ocean Sciences, National Science Foundation; Cindy Stong, Professor of
Marine Biology, Bowling Green State University; Mr. Maxwell Cohen; and
the staffs at the National Aquarium, Baltimore; the Thames Science Center,
New London, Connecticut; and the American Museum of Natural History.*

To Margo, Bruce, Emily, and Beth, with love
J.C.

For Mom and Dad and summer days at the beach
B.D.

It was the end of the day,
and it was *hot* in school.
We had been working for hours
on our ocean science projects.
All our work made Ms. Frizzle very happy.
But it made *us* very tired and hot.

WOW. IT'S HOT TODAY.

NOT MS. FRIZZLE'S DRESS.

YEAH, IT'S COOL, MAN.

OIL SPILL

DAILY BUZZ

PROTECT OUR OCEANS SCRAPBOOK by Wanda and Phil

Children Help Clean Up Beach

OCEANS SAY: STOP USING US AS A GARBAGE CAN

Plastics trap Sea Animals

MODELS OF SEA URCHINS by Gregory
I made these out of clay and toothpicks.

Sea urchins crawl on the sea bottom. They eat plants. They have sharp spikes to protect them.

This is a picture of a sea urchin

9

SWIMMERS IN THE SEA
by Shirley, John and Ralph

FISH - Sweeps tail from side to side

WHALE Moves tail up and down

JELLYFISH - Opens body like an umbrella, then closes rapidly to jet upward

SQUID - takes in water and forces it out to jet forward or backward

SCALLOP ~ opens and closes shell rapidly to move.

This is my sculpture of a HUMUHUMUNUKUNUKUAPUAA
A FISH THAT LIVES IN HAWAII
(THE NAME IS LONGER THAN THE FISH)
—ALEX

We were putting the finishing touches on a display about how ocean animals swim when someone said, "I wish *we* could go swimming."

Chart of uncharted seas.

Ms. Frizzle looked up.
Without warning, she said,
"As a matter of fact, children,
I've been planning a class trip to the ocean
for tomorrow."
Everybody cheered.
Sometimes having a weird teacher isn't so bad!

DID SHE SAY OCEAN?

WHERE WE CAN SWIM AND PLAY?

IS SHE SERIOUS?

DON'T ASK, JUST PACK YOUR BEACH BAG!

WHY IS THE OCEAN SALTY?
by Tim
Much of the salt in the ocean water comes from rocks. Rocks have salt in them. When rocks are worn down by water, the salt goes into the water.

SALT 1 LB.   SALT 1 LB.

One cubic foot of seawater has over 2 pounds of salt in it.

MOST OF THE SALT IN THE OCEAN IS THE SAME KIND WE PUT ON FOOD.

SALADS   HOT LUNCH

11

The next day, everyone showed up
in a bathing suit.
We boarded the old school bus,
and Frizzie started the engine.
We were ready for a day of
fun in the sun!

I CAN'T WAIT TO GO SWIMMING!

I'M GOING TO BUILD A SAND CASTLE.

BOY, ARE WE LUCKY!

When we finally came to the beach,
we wanted to jump off the bus.
But guess what?
Ms. Frizzle didn't stop.
She kept right on going —
past the lifeguard station,
across the sand,
and down to the water's edge.

WHERE DOES SAND COME FROM?
by Phoebe

Sand is formed when rocks break apart and crumble into bits. Each grain of sand is really a tiny piece of rock or shell.

HI! I'M LENNY THE LIFEGUARD. HERE'S A PICTURE OF ME SAVING A THIRD-GRADER LAST SUMMER.

Mm-Hm

HEY, WHERE ARE WE GOING?

ISN'T SHE SUPPOSED TO PARK IN THE PARKING LOT?

Mm-Hm

LENNY'S LIFEGUARD SCRAPBOOK

LIFEGUARD

WIND, SAND, AND STARFISH

13

TIDES RISE AND FALL
EVERY DAY
by Rachel

When the water near shore rises and gets deep, it is high tide.
When the water falls and gets shallow, it is low tide.

HIGH TIDE   LOW TIDE

Tides are caused mostly by the pull of the moon's gravity on the earth and its oceans.

"We are now in the intertidal zone," said Ms. Frizzle.
"That is the part of shore that is covered with water at high tide, and uncovered at low tide."

HERE I AM SAVING A GRANDMOTHER... AND THIS IS MY FAMOUS RESCUE OF MUFFY, A BELOVED FAMILY PET.

MM-HM

MM-HM

Out the windows we saw tide pools —
puddles of water left on shore
when the tide goes out.
We were hoping the Friz would let us out,
but no such luck.
She kept driving full speed ahead.

WE ARE HERE

TIDE POOL
HIGH TIDE
LOW TIDE
INTERTIDAL ZONE

SS SCHOOL BUS

SHE SAID WE WERE GOING TO THE BEACH.

NO, SHE DIDN'T. SHE SAID WE WERE GOING TO THE OCEAN.

I GUESS SHE REALLY MEANT IT!

Periwinkles

Seaweeds

Sea Stars

Limpets

Mussels

Green Crabs

Barnacles

Sea Urchins

15

WHAT MAKES WAVES?
by Florrie

Most of the waves we see are caused by wind. The stronger the wind, the bigger the waves.

A BREEZE MAKES LITTLE RIPPLES.

A STRONG WIND MAKES LARGE WAVES.

As the bus splashed through the waves,
the lifeguard blew his whistle.
Frizzie didn't stop,
so he came rushing out to rescue us.

PARDON ME, PLEASE. I HAVE TO RESCUE A SCHOOL BUS.

MM-HM

MM-MM

Suddenly a mysterious wave rose up.
Ms. Frizzle opened the door of the bus,
and the lifeguard was swept inside.
Outside the windows
we saw nothing but rushing water.
We screamed and closed our eyes.

17

When we finally opened our eyes,
everything was quiet.
We were under the ocean,
and there had been a few small changes.
The bus had turned into a submarine,
and everyone was wearing a diving suit.
We should have known.
We were on another one of Ms. Frizzle's
crazy class trips!

Right away, Ms. Frizzle started talking about the ocean.

"We are now passing over the continental shelf," she said. "That's the area that stretches from the shore to where the water is four hundred to six hundred feet deep."

WHAT IS THE CONTINENTAL SHELF?
by Carmen

All around the edge of the world's continents, the land slants down and is covered by ocean water. This underwater land is called the continental shelf.

CLASS, THE WATER IS GETTING DEEPER AND DEEPER.

OCEAN SCIENCE IS TOO DEEP FOR ME!

FISHY

Grunts

A NEW WORD
by Dorothy Ann

A **continent** is one of the seven main masses of land on the earth.

1. Africa
2. Antarctica
3. Asia
4. Australia
5. Europe
6. North America
7. South America

WE ARE HERE
CONTINENTAL SHELF
S.S. SCHOOL BUS

HOW CAN FISH BREATHE
UNDERWATER?
        by Amanda Jane
People have lungs that
take oxygen from air.
Fish have gills that
can take oxygen from water

OXYGEN
DISSOLVED IN WATER

WATER

WATER

GILLS TAKE
IN OXYGEN

WATER
PASSES THROUGH

Water flows into the
fish's mouth,
then the gills, and out
through slits in the
fish's sides.

Ms. Frizzle decided this was a good moment
for us to get out of the bus.
Thank goodness we had air tanks!
All around us were fish, fish, and more fish.
"Many kinds of fish swim in large groups
called *schools*," said Ms. Frizzle.

Sponges

LOOK!
A SCHOOL
OF FISH!

LOOK!
A SCHOOL OF
CHILDREN!

I WISH
WE HAD
A BUS.

Down below, on the muddy bottom,
lobsters were catching crabs.
Starfish used their arms
to pry open clamshells.
And jellyfish floated past,
catching small fish
with their stinging tentacles.
The ocean was teeming with life!

Medusa Jellyfish

MOST OF THE SEAFOOD
WE EAT COMES FROM HERE
ON THE CONTINENTAL SHELF,
ARNOLD.

I THOUGHT IT CAME
FROM THE
SUPERMARKET SHELF.

Blue Crab

Lobster

WHELKS

Sea Star

Clam

Blue Scallops

Q: WHEN IS A FISH
NOT A FISH?
A: WHEN IT'S A JELLYFISH!
by Gregory
A true fish has a
backbone, gills and fins.
Some animals are
called "fish" but they
are not. Actually, they
are invertebrates, animals
without backbones.

Here are some of them:

Jellyfish

Sea Star
(also called starfish)

shellfish

SCALLOP   MUSSEL   SNAIL   CRAB

WHAT IS PLANKTON?
by Arnold

Plankton is a mass of plants and animals that float near the surface of the ocean. Most plankton are very small. Many cannot be seen without a microscope.

Ms. Frizzle said there was
life in the water
we couldn't even see.
She pulled out a microscope
and made us look at seawater.
Under the microscope we saw strange creatures.
"Girls and boys," said Ms. Frizzle,
"these tiny living things are called *plankton*."

We tried to listen, but we felt nervous. We noticed some dark shapes coming closer and closer.

WHERE HAVE I SEEN THAT SCARY SHAPE BEFORE?

DOES THE WORD SHARK MEAN ANYTHING TO YOU?

OH NO! CHILDREN SHOULD NOT BE SWIMMING IN SHARK-INFESTED WATERS.

THANKS FOR THE SAFETY TIP, LENNY.

HOW THE SUN FEEDS OCEAN ANIMALS
by John

Plankton plants make food by using energy from the sun. Plankton animals eat the plankton plants. Larger animals eat the plankton animals. This is called a food chain. Without the sun shining on plankton plants most ocean animals could not exist.

A FOOD CHAIN

LARGE FISH eat MIDDLE-SIZE FISH eat SMALL FISH eat TINY WATER ANIMALS eat MICROSCOPIC PLANKTON

23

SHARKS ARE FISH
by Molly
Most sharks are fast swimmers with razor-sharp teeth. Usually they eat ocean animals like crabs, fish, seals— even other sharks.

SOME KINDS OF SHARKS

GREAT WHITE →

← HAMMERHEAD

THRESHER →

NURSE →

A DIFFERENT KIND OF SKELETON
by Ralph
Sharks do not have bones like other fish. Their skeleton is made of cartilage. This is the same bendable material that is in your ears and the tip of your nose.

Oh, no! The shapes were tiger sharks!
Ms. Frizzle told us not to worry.
She said most sharks will not eat people.
"The number of people killed by sharks every year is very, very small,"
said Ms. Frizzle.
We panicked anyway!

Tiger Sharks

HUMANS ARE NOT THE MAIN DIET OF TIGER SHARKS BUT THEY MAY ATTACK IF HUMANS ARE NEARBY.

UH-OH! WE'RE NEARBY!

Then an enormous whale shark slid by.
"Whale sharks never hurt people.
They eat nothing but plankton,"
said Ms. Frizzle.
The giant shark swam down, and we went along.
We were leaving the continental shelf, following
a steep cliff called the continental slope.
We were on our way to the deep ocean floor.

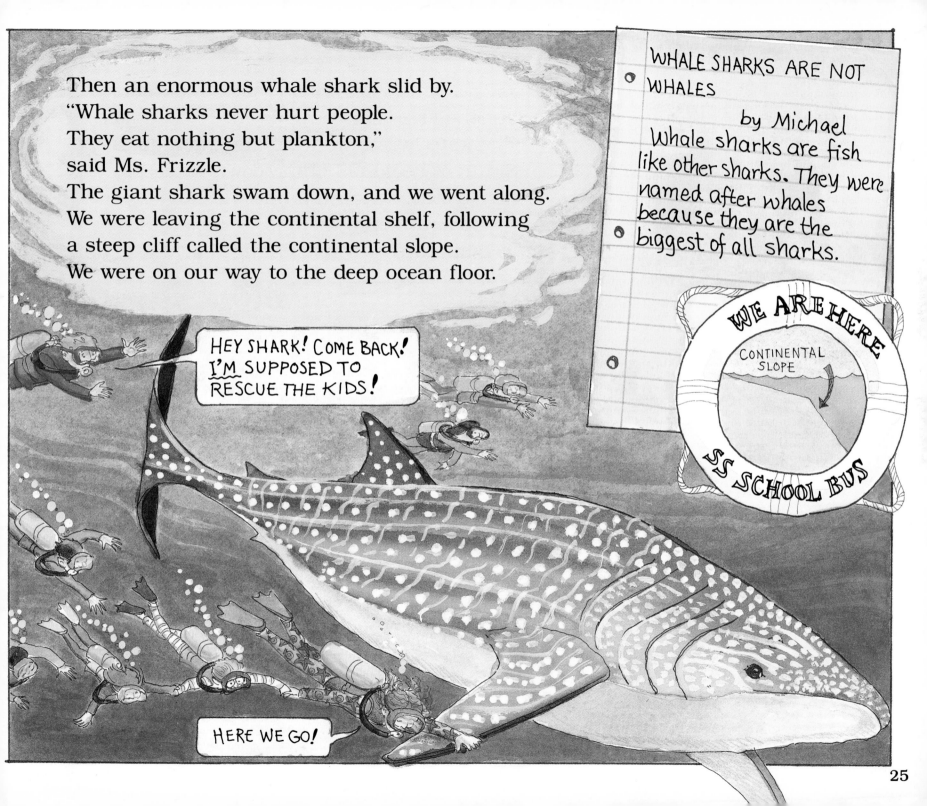

WHALE SHARKS ARE NOT WHALES

by Michael

Whale sharks are fish like other sharks. They were named after whales because they are the biggest of all sharks.

HEY SHARK! COME BACK! I'M SUPPOSED TO RESCUE THE KIDS!

WE ARE HERE

CONTINENTAL SLOPE

SS SCHOOL BUS

HERE WE GO!

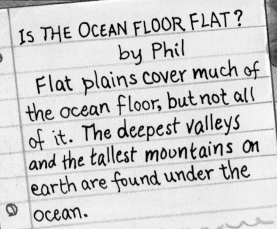

IS THE OCEAN FLOOR FLAT?
by Phil
Flat plains cover much of the ocean floor, but not all of it. The deepest valleys and the tallest mountains on earth are found under the ocean.

An Underwater Valley is called a trench ↓

The deepest trench yet found is 7 miles down

ISLANDS ARE MOUNTAINTOPS
by Arnold
When the top of an under-sea mountain is above the surface, it is called an island.

LOOK! AN ISLAND!

LOOK! A MOUNTAIN!

After a while, the whale shark swam away, but the Friz kept going down.
The water was bitter cold and pitch-dark.
Sunlight could not shine down so deep.
Ms. Frizzle switched on her flashlight.
As we swam onto the bus,
we noticed that it had changed again.

YOU'RE NOT AFRAID OF THE DARK, ARE YOU, ARNOLD?

WHO ME? I LOVE THE DARK. THE DARK IS MY FRIEND. CAN WE GO HOME NOW?

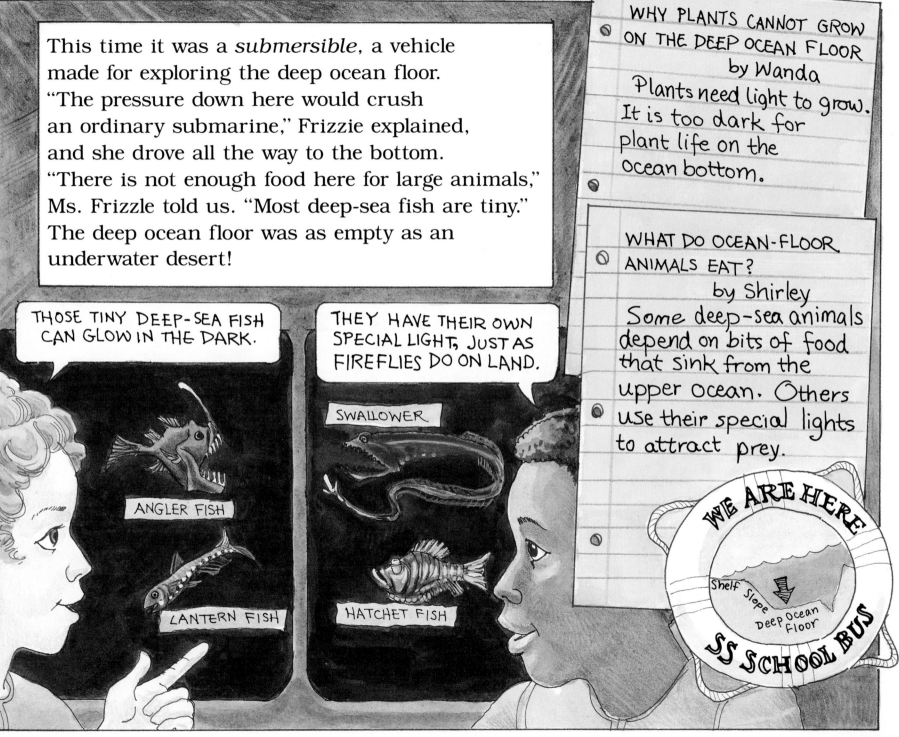

This time it was a *submersible,* a vehicle made for exploring the deep ocean floor. "The pressure down here would crush an ordinary submarine," Frizzie explained, and she drove all the way to the bottom. "There is not enough food here for large animals," Ms. Frizzle told us. "Most deep-sea fish are tiny." The deep ocean floor was as empty as an underwater desert!

THOSE TINY DEEP-SEA FISH CAN GLOW IN THE DARK.

THEY HAVE THEIR OWN SPECIAL LIGHT, JUST AS FIREFLIES DO ON LAND.

ANGLER FISH

LANTERN FISH

SWALLOWER

HATCHET FISH

WHY PLANTS CANNOT GROW ON THE DEEP OCEAN FLOOR
by Wanda
Plants need light to grow. It is too dark for plant life on the ocean bottom.

WHAT DO OCEAN-FLOOR ANIMALS EAT?
by Shirley
Some deep-sea animals depend on bits of food that sink from the upper ocean. Others use their special lights to attract prey.

WE ARE HERE
SS SCHOOL BUS
Shelf
Slope
Deep Ocean Floor

WHAT CAUSES ...
by Alex
A vent is formed when
seawater seeps into cracks
in the ocean floor. The
water touches super-hot
rocks inside the earth.
Then the hot water shoots
up out of the vent.

WATER

LAVA

HOW FOOD IS MADE AT A VENT
by Shirley
Special bacteria
manufacture their own
food using heat energy
and hydrogen sulfide gas
from the vent. This food
supports much of the
life at the vent.

Then up ahead, we saw a spot that was full of life.
It looked like an undersea garden with all kinds
of strange animals in it.
"This is a hot-water *vent*, class," said the Friz.
"A vent is an opening in the ocean floor.
Flowing from the vent is super-hot water
mixed with hydrogen sulfide gas."

AT A HOT-WATER VENT THERE IS
ENOUGH FOOD FOR MANY LARGE
ANIMALS.

THESE TUBE WORMS
LOOK LIKE HUGE LIPSTICKS.

HUGE CLAMS (1 FOOT OR MORE)

GIANT TUBE WORMS (8 TO 10 FEET)

Ms. Frizzle said there were other vents
on the ocean floor.
"Unfortunately, we don't have time
to visit them," she added.
Then she pulled up a lever on the dashboard,
and the bus zoomed toward the surface.

THOSE WORMS LOOK JUST LIKE SPAGHETTI.

DID WE HAVE LUNCH?

PLEASE. I JUST LOST MY APPETITE.

THAT DANDELION ANIMAL IS LIKE A LITTLE FLOWER!

DANDELION ANIMAL (2 INCHES)

BLIND CRABS AND SHRIMP (UP TO 1 FOOT)

MATS OF BACTERIA (30 INCHES THICK)

SPAGHETTI WORMS (UP TO 2-3 feet)

WHEN THE FIRST VENTS WERE FOUND
by JOHN
The first vents were discovered in the 1970's and 1980's. Before then, Ocean scientists had never seen large animals like these on the deep ocean floor.

HOW IS A CORAL REEF BUILT?
by Amanda Jane

Each coral polyp grows a stony skeleton around itself. The reef is made of a layer of living coral animals attached to a wall of many millions of dead skeletons.

Actual sizes of typical coral polyps

Each "pock mark" is a single coral animal.

HOW CORAL POLYPS EAT
by Rachel

Most corals feed at night. Tiny arms come out of a coral's stony skeleton. The arms catch plankton and pass it into the coral's mouth.

MOUTH

ARMS

SKELETON

CORAL POLYP IN THE DAYTIME

THE SAME POLYP AT NIGHT

Soon we were motoring over the open ocean toward a sun-drenched island.
The bus had changed into a glass-bottom boat.
Through the glass, we saw what looked like a wall made of colorful rocks.
Ms. Frizzle said it was a coral reef, made of tiny animals called coral *polyps*.
We dove overboard and began to explore.

The reef was made of many different kinds of corals.
Some looked like trees with branches.
Others looked like fans or fingers.
Some even looked like human brains!

THREE KINDS OF CORAL REEFS
by Tim

1. A fringing reef is attached to the shore.

TOP VIEW   SIDE VIEW
          REEF

2. A barrier reef has a channel of water between it and the shore.
          WATER

3. An atoll is a ring of coral around a sunken volcano.
          SUNKEN VOLCANO

WE ARE HERE
ISLAND
FRINGING REEF
MS. FRIZZLE AND THE KIDS ARE ON A FRINGING REEF ATTACHED TO THE SHORE OF AN ISLAND.
BUS

32

"A coral reef makes a good home
for many ocean plants and animals,"
said the Friz.
We saw crabs and lobsters,
huge eels and octopuses,
slimy sea slugs and spiny sea urchins,
and the most colorful fish in the world.

SMILE, EVERYONE!

I ALWAYS KNEW I WAS A STAR.

MORAY EEL

GIANT CLAM

SEA HARE

Too soon, Ms. Frizzle said it was time to go.
No one wanted to be left behind
so we all climbed aboard.
Frizzie stepped on the gas,
and the bus chugged away from the coral reef.

MAMMALS IN THE SEA
by Florrie

Animals such as dolphins, whales, seals and walruses are not fish. They are warm-blooded mammals like horses, dogs and human beings.

Most fish lay eggs but mammals do not. Mother mammals give birth to live young and feed their babies with milk.

Nearby, a school of dolphins leaped past.
In the distance, we saw a whale.
Everything seemed normal.
Then we noticed that something weird was happening.
The bus was getting *flat.*

HI! I'M A MAMMAL.

SMALL WORLD ISN'T IT? SO ARE WE!

SEAL

DOLPHIN

WHALE

WALRUS

SEA COW

SEA OTTER

SPERM WHALE

BOTTLENOSE DOLPHINS

WE ARE HERE
OPEN OCEAN
SS SCHOOL BUS

As usual, Ms. Frizzle was the only one who stayed calm.
She drove us to an ocean current, and we were swept along in the fast-moving water for thousands of miles.
After a while, we saw our beach again.

TELL ME, KIDS, IS YOUR BUS ALWAYS LIKE THIS?

WELL IT'S NEVER BEEN A BOAT BEFORE...

AND IT'S NEVER BEEN FLAT BEFORE...

BUT OTHERWISE IT HASN'T CHANGED.

KEEP YOUR BALANCE, CLASS.

RIVERS IN THE OCEAN
by Phoebe
Parts of the ocean flow like rivers. These moving areas are called ocean currents.

WHY DO BIG WAVES "BREAK" NEAR SHORE?
by Carmen

In shallow water, the ocean bottom drags on the lower part of the wave and slows it down. The upper part keeps going fast, so it falls over, or breaks.

TOP KEEPS GOING FAST

BOTTOM SLOWS DOWN

"Everyone stay on the bus!" shouted the Friz.
On the bus was right.
It had turned into a giant surfboard!

THIS IS THE GREATEST RESCUE OF MY CAREER.

CONGRATULATIONS, LENNY!

WE KNEW YOU COULD DO IT!

PELICANS

We had to stand on top of it.
And we were riding a wild wave
straight toward shore!

Oh, no! It was a giant wipeout!
The whole class went under.
The next thing we knew,
we were washing up on the sand.

Our diving suits were gone,
and the bus was its old self again.
There it was, sitting in the parking lot
as if nothing had happened.
We thanked Lenny for everything
and hit the road.

Back in our classroom,
we made a terrific chart of the ocean
for the bulletin board.

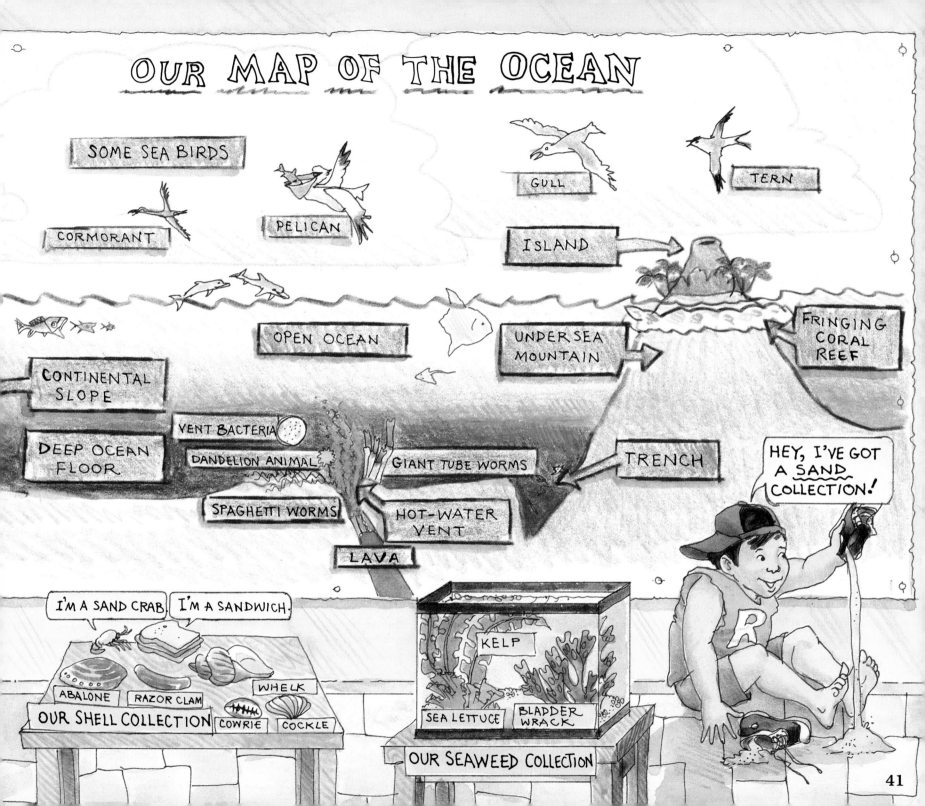

By then we were definitely ready to go home.
Thank goodness it was Friday!
After that class trip
we really *needed* a weekend off!

43

MULTIPLE-CHOICE TEST

FIND OUT WHICH THINGS ARE TRUE, AND WHICH THINGS ARE MAKE-BELIEVE!

First, read the question. Then read the three answers — A, B, and C. Decide which one is correct. To see if you were right, check the answers on the next page.

QUESTIONS:

1. In real life, what would happen if a school bus drove into the ocean?
  A. The bus would turn into a submarine, then a submersible, then a glass-bottom boat, and finally, a surfboard.
  B. The bus would stay a bus.
  C. The bus would turn into a rubber-ducky.

2. Is it possible to explore the ocean in a single day?
  A. Yes, if you travel by giant clam.
  B. No, you couldn't do it in a day. It would take months, no matter how you made the trip.
  C. Maybe. It depends on how long the day is.

3. In real life, can ocean animals speak?
  A. Yes, but only when they have something important to say.
  B. Yes, but too many bubbles come out.
  C. No. Ocean animals do not talk.

ANSWERS:

1. The correct answer is B. A bus cannot magically change into anything else. It also cannot run under the ocean. Water would seep inside and the bus would sink.

2. The correct answer is B. It takes a long time to travel thousands of miles through water. Even whales need months to migrate from one part of the ocean to another.

3. The correct answer is C. It is true that many fish make sounds, and whales and dolphins seem to communicate in a special way. But ocean animals do not use human language, and no one has ever heard a sea star tell a joke.